I AM YOU

TortoisWind

"Judge not lest ye be judged."
Matthew 7:1

I AM YOU
Copyright © 2015 by TortoisWind

Printed in USA
www.tortoiswind.com
www.iamyou.life
tortoiswind@gmail.com

In Loving Memory of:

My Grandparents,
May they continue to rest in Heaven

Vannoy "The Wire Man" Streeter
Ezella Marie Streeter (McClain)
Cleveland Brown III
Carrie Brown (Payton)

Also, two beautiful women that I was honored to
know for a short amount of time but experienced
an amazing relationship with before God called
them home – they touched many lives including
mine:
Mrs. Rose Mary Smith
Mrs. Erika Rowan-O'Neal

Dedication

I prayed for these words and the Lord has granted me what I asked of Him. So now, I return these words to you Lord, dedicating this book inspired by your love back to the Heavens.

Intro – Induction 〰

Before I reveal to you who I am and before I discover who you are, please take this moment and reflect on life. You must be humble enough to not be offended when you realize that I am you and you are me.

This moment, right now, is about us.

These moments are not mine as individuals but a collection of experiences perceived from my point of view - not of me, not of you, but of this entire existence. I am me because you are you and together we define our mind's logic, our body's limitations, and our soul's purpose, releasing the truth in its purest form.

Believe that you are understood and this collection of thoughts is proof that I know you even if, you do not know me. By the end of this experience you will realize that you have complete understanding of the beginning. You will become aware that your beginning is your end. It starts with me and ends with you, as the unknown becomes known. Just accept that I know who you are because I know that I am you and we are the key to freedom.

A Moment of Bliss 〜〜

From My True Love:

"I have it all planned out. Plans to take care of you not abandon you. Plans to give you the future you hope for. When you call on Me, when you come and pray to Me, I will listen. When you come looking for Me, you will find Me. Yes when you get serious about finding Me and want it more than anything else, I will make sure you are not disappointed...I will turn things around for you."

(Jeremiah 29:11-14, The Holy Bible)

I am you.

If you Think it is Possible to be Lost, then you Suffer 〰

When you don't know what to do with yourself, what do you do? Another day that I rise but I do not shine. I am searching everywhere to see a glimpse of light, to feel the slightest vibration, and yet, I find nothing. The thoughts of bills, loneliness, and failure suffocate any positive energy that I have. I have never encountered this many feelings at once. My mind has been contaminated with emotions.

I am striving every day to be on top. I am fighting to project the true me, but I am lost. I have trapped my hero inside myself and it is dark in here. I thought I would find happiness outside of myself. I went to college. That didn't define me. I pursued a career in Corporate America. That didn't define me. I am a mother

8

and though it is a true projection of me, it does not define me. No lover has come close to defining me and religion has defied me more than defined me. The more I pour my heart and soul into these facets of life, the more it is revealed that I am not happy.

I allowed the ones that I knew I could live without, to slip away. Now, I sit here in my bare bones, down to the minimal, my projections. I attempt to guide them in a different direction. Yet, it is impossible to live through a vessel that is not completely filled with your own spirit. The essence of your spirit begins its journey dwelling inside of your given vessel but it is still free and that should always be respected. I try to guide without manipulating such impressionable beings. As I back off, I fall deeper into myself, lost in a forest where every tree looks the same and every path, that appears to be the way home, just leads me further and further into nothingness. A place where every day is the same no matter what I do. So, I choose to do nothing.

I scream loud from frustration but my screams go unheard. Cliché forms of empathy, sympathy, encouragement, and so called, motivations are thrown at me. I can see each letter of each word spoken dancing around me, above me, and beneath me, but none of these words could penetrate my soul.

These words lack light. I do not truly see them. They lack vibration. I do not truly feel them. They lack truth. I cannot accept them. They lack wisdom. I do not understand them. These are words that I do not know. At this point of my existence, they are just words. If the tongue that releases these words has no power, then the words have no power. Speaking alone does not give me power. It is when I am seen, heard, felt, enlightened, and accepted that power exists. For now, I am exercising my right to remain silent and to remain in silence.

This journey to be on top is long and complicated. It feels damn near impossible. Which version of me will flourish until the end, exposing herself as greatness and taking her rightful spot, showing this world who she really is? So many have tried and so many have failed. I do know if she exists and if she is fighting to be born again. Will the forest consume me or will I be rescued? I trust her to commit to the quest and I will continue to sit here and wait patiently for my hero, my Goddess, my power.

Now, I vibrate.

The Day after the Full Moon

We exist with the same gravitational forces that cause the tides to rise high, destroy masses of land, and snatch the breath from every living thing in its path. This same force, only hours later, will tickle the toes of a two year old experiencing the ocean front for the very first time. The day after the full moon is dictated by the gravitational effects of the moon, the sun, and the rotation of the earth, which create a force so great, yet so gentle. The same clouds that were white just hours ago appear dark in comparison to the moon. Clouds, whether dark or white, shield the earth from the light; a shield that we beg for during the heat of the day and regret in the midst of the night.

Imagine floating on a raft in the middle of the ocean. During the day the sun is blinding and scorches the flesh, draining your energy. You beg for the clouds to show themselves, to be your shield, to protect you from the light, so you can see your way to safety. The light is so piercing that you can only absorb it.

Your eyes are so sensitive to the light that you must shut them. You still cannot find darkness and at this moment. You crave to be in the dark because seeing the light brings you pain. The universe obliges you and sends the beautiful white fluffy clouds to give you relief from the light; now you may see. Your eyes regain focus and you see an ocean of waves flowing to the same rhythm. You and your heart become hypnotized. You concentrate on the pattern of waves that are reflecting the same sun that just blinded you. You concentrate on the moon that commands the waves to destroy you. You concentrate on the earth that will not stand still. The three allies, the sun, the moon, and the earth, conspire to control you.

Now the sun is setting, the moon is rising, and darkness is settling all around you. This darkness introduces itself in the absence of the light. Your eyes begin to adjust and the reflection of the sun onto the moon becomes a guide instead of a blinding force. You begin to appreciate the sun and the light it left behind as it aids the moon in giving you sight. The waves are not as hypnotizing to the eyes but now your ears are fully concentrated on the rhythm. A nice steady flow gives you comfort but large splashes begin to disrupt your peace allowing the unknown to place fear in your heart. The same clouds that you made your ally during the day are now your enemy throughout the night. Your protection from the light is now your predator's aide which allows you to now be hunted during the night. Your desires have changed because the shield is now blocking the only light that exists. The darkness smothers you, seducing your consciousness, slowly causing you to sleep with your eyes wide open.

The sounds of the waves give off clues as to which type of moon lies behind the shield of the dark clouds. A full moon produces the highest of the tides but also gives you the most light. When the moon is at first or third quarter, then the high tides will be at their lowest. So, which do you prefer? Does preference even matter when you have no control over the sun or the moon? The earth will continue to rotate on its axis. The sun will continue to rise and set. The moon will go through the twelve phases no matter what your position in this universe. What do you control? Must you simply learn to adapt to change, like the tides?

I was stuck in the middle of the ocean on a raft trying to defeat the sun, the moon, and the earth. The more I tried to go against the natural state of life, the more I lost myself. Then, the day came. I decided to just slide off the raft into the ocean and give up hope of finding a different life. I closed my eyes and slowly counted down from 10 to 1 seeing each number appear before me. I became engulfed in black and became the shield.

Now that I am the shield of this alternate universe, I begin to experience a light that cannot be seen by the world. I can see the light and I can block others from the light. I am in control. I mastered experiencing the dark and the light simultaneously. I am all things that allow me to experience peace in spite of my circumstances.

Reflections of an Aquarius 〰〰

I don't know why I let go this time, why I allowed him to enter my peace. It was our routine, here today - gone tomorrow. He taught me a lot about myself. He was the only one who loved me enough to let me go. Usually, relationships end because of disagreements and misunderstandings. Our relationship never ends. It evolves. As soon as I master the skill he is teaching, the experience quickly comes to an end and a new one begins. Each lesson is necessary for my existence. I have mastered survival and I have conquered fear. My confidence is soaring. I am divine. I can exist in the dark and in the light. I fear nothing and no one. I accept the truths handed down from the Great One and collect wisdom from an infinite number of beings. I am closer to my destiny. I can feel it. My training is almost complete.

After many years of war, my warrior is back. The vibration of his energy is so strong. That will never change. We stare into each other's eyes and rest in each other's essence. He has been gone for what feels like centuries but his essence always resonates in my soul. In my universe, he never left. He is always with my soul which allows him to forever come back to me. As we read each other's thoughts, I stumble upon an unfamiliar place in his mind. The door isn't new; I can tell by the architecture. But, it is new to me. He can feel me wondering in this new place. His spirit embraces me and we both stand in front of the door. I can feel his energy vibrating even faster. I am not sure if I should match him. The energy is so powerful. In order to open the door to this tunnel, I have to match his frequency. He has always harnessed and protected my energy and has never led me astray.

In all of my existence, I have never hesitated walking through a new door. This moment is different. I am not afraid and I know I can survive anything but this isn't a test of those skills. Immortality waits on the other side. It is time to evolve, time to establish my families' legacy. Why now? The Great One has been my guide throughout this journey and now, I am supposed to walk through a door without instructions?

I have one foot in and one foot out. I am indecisive and that is not familiar to me. I thrive on impulse just following the moment. He can feel my indecisiveness. He is known for weighing choices on his great scale and revealing which option holds more weight. As I search his eyes for answers to see the results from the scale, I notice something that rarely happens...the scale is balanced. I did not know how to respond. I share an amazing kiss with this mighty King. As our tongues dance to his strong vibrations, our hands caress each other's souls. I open my eyes to see the scale and right before I glance into his world he grabs my heart and opens the door. His eyes lure me right over the threshold.

There is no turning back. The universe surrounds us. We made the world disappear again. The tunnel keeps us discreet. It is him, the one my soul longs for, and his presence is so much more relaxed than mine. We are in pure nothingness. There is a creative essence in the tunnel. His breath blows over my neck like a soft, cool breeze coming off the ocean. His kisses penetrate my crown allowing me to access his mind. Our communication is telepathic. As I enter his thoughts, our bodies respond naturally creating the oneness that we each long for every moment of our existence. I feel his breath travel from my neck to my breast. His pulse is in tune with mine. I am reading his mind as he exposes the road he is travelling to reach his treasure. This is a totally new experience, travelling the tunnel with any being, let alone a King. For the first time, I will enter into the unknown accompanied by my knight in shining armor.

Just the thought alone sends my vibrations galactically. Everything in existence is being affected by my Aquarius energy. Every being in existence must be experiencing internal bliss.

I can feel the next destination getting closer. My vibrations begin to slow down on their own. I know that we will be visiting a dense environment. My spirit materializes. I reach for what should be his hand but I am only grasping at air. He does not vibrate low. He does not matter. I cannot experience him in the flesh. I want one last kiss before I leave the tunnel. It is evident that he will not be joining me for this mission. I gaze into his eyes and I search for his soul. Just like that, he is gone. No goodbyes yet again - another solo mission. Maybe we will cross each other's paths in another lifetime or maybe, just maybe, he waits for me on the other side of this door. I hope that I am travelling to a world filled with peace and joy. I need a vacation...

As my physical self, pieces itself together, I can feel her, my warrior spirit. I sense war up ahead. Whom shall I fight this time?

War of the Mind 〜〜

I am addicted to marijuana and playing the lottery. I used to get out and grind so that I would not have to keep slaving from 8am to 5pm for pennies on the hour. I went to college and got a piece of paper which will probably be the reason my part time check is garnished. That is hilarious to me because again, it is my fault. I made a hasty decision to take out a student loan, even though, I had scholarships. The credit card company probably has a fucking lean against a house I don't live in but pay for with every penny I can scrape together. Memphis, Tennessee, a city I moved to in the name of love.

A city that seduced me the moment I entered her. The only problem, I loved the person I was moving for more than he loved me. He claimed he was in love but he was already cheating on me before I even packed the first bag. Everyone knew this except me. Do you want to know what love decided to do? Love allowed a single mother and her son to move four hours away from every support system they had to come to a place where love never had any intention of taking care of them. But again, that was my fault. I turned a blind eye to every red flag that was waved in my face. However, I did take notes. It didn't last a year and my ego would not let me move back home. I lost my man. I lost my job. I lost my apartment. My psyche was so fucked up; I thought I had lost my mind. I have to give myself a little credit. I didn't run back to him. Then again, it wasn't really an option. Truth is, after I found out he was disloyal and he moved out, my son and I no longer existed to him. Now, the only support system I had in this foreign land was me and a projection of me.

I never would have pieced this life together. I sacrifice important things and get bullshit in return. Today, I declare war against myself. I must literally, be going insane because I keep doing the same thing expecting the results to change. I keep trying to fit this square peg through this triangle door and no matter how I adjust it, squeeze it, and push it, it just will not fit! My life is upside down. I have a few kids by a few men and this shit is bananas. I gave up on cussing and fussing with them a long time ago. I try my hardest just to not say anything. I have tons of debt haunting me. I guess I fell for the trap. Who would have thought I would have married a man I met behind bars, and hell no, it didn't last! Me - this is my life. I have to own every agreement that I made in this universe. I think I have been waiting on some outside source to come and save me, to rescue me from all of this madness, but this person or thing does not exist.

I feel like I am being unfair if I try to blame everyone else.

I could blame the first guy that broke my heart for all of my failed relationships. I could say that his cheating on me brought about all my insecurities. If a man is not in my sight, then I just assume he is with another woman and for me that has been somewhat true. I am so far from being "myself," that technically; he is with a different woman every time he is in the presence of my physical being. My body is the same but he is experiencing a different spirit every day. The sweet, soft, gentle, and loving spirit that he once knew could not withstand the pain of his disloyalty. I now deal with separation issues. I go above and beyond for love. I try to make his life so convenient that it should be easily understood; I am the last person he needs to worry about letting him down. But, in the process, I never feel like the love is reciprocated on the same frequency. I don't want to continue like this. These cycles just keep coming around and around. I do not know why I cannot pass this test.

It was suggested that it may have stemmed from being the child of a military man who was gone a lot while I was growing up. I guess I wasn't really raised in a two parent home. It was just a two income home. Here I am; here I stand with these kids and a limited income. I can honestly say I am not doing much at this exact moment to change my situation because I do not know how.

I never cried so much in my life. I had never been that alone in all my existence. My son was in kindergarten at the time. It was too much. I just realized that this happened 11 years ago and after two more kids, the story is not much different. I see a pattern that has me on a path to self-destruction. Fuck that. I say the obvious; I have to do better for my kids. The truth is, right now, I have to do better for me then my kids will reap the harvest.

Looking For Love 〜〜

I thought I found love in all the wrong
places. I have been programmed to search
outside of myself.

Believe me, I have searched long and hard.
My issue is patience. All my life, I have made
decisions based on impulse. I just do things
because at the moment it feels right; never really
weighing my options. I have allowed loneliness
to kick my ass. Loneliness has a hold on me so
tight that I have convinced myself I want to be
alone. I am so terrified of love. I feel like men
only pretend to love me so they can get what
they need from life at that moment. They are

vampires and I am all out of blood. I have worked so hard to re-up on energy. The little bit that I get, I quickly allow another vampire to feed off my supply. When I am all out and messed up, I cannot feed from the same beings that fed off of me. This is where the marijuana comes into play. Now, I need an outside source to get back to the tunnel. Sometimes, it's cool and the experience is refreshing. Other times, I am just surrounded by darkness because I made the universe disappear again. The thing that rattles my mind is how much I appreciate the dark more than the light. Why is this? My light attracts all the darkness. I need to attract more light, so that I can expand in this lifetime and not fade away. But, slowly, I am fading into the black. My light is dimming and if I don't snap out of this, I will condense down to nothing and blend in with the rest of the world. Everything in me knows that I am supposed to change this world and not let it change me.

Condensing 〰

As I glance at the scoreboard, I can clearly
see that I am losing and there is not much time
left on the clock. I am trying to hang in there
and keep going strong. But, I am not
conditioned well enough to last much longer. I
know physically, I am not up for the challenge.
This vessel is worn and my mind is not as sharp
as it needs to be. Right now, I only have faith in
my spirit and I am about to find out just how
strong it is.

I have to make a decision. I am not sure how
long I have been in the tunnel but I know, that
very soon, I am going to have to face reality.

29

The instructions are simple. My new mission is to simply detach from the beings that are draining my energies. This covers people, circumstances, and ideologies. It is time to embrace the third dimension and seek the truth, the beauty, and the freedom that exists in this realm contrary to popular belief. So many illusions to dig through, but just like a diamond in the rough, these precious jewels exist within this dimension. They are hard to see with the naked eye but I have been sent so that they may be seen and the wonders of their souls will be uncovered. The transformation begins, when the scales are balanced. I will use the darkness as my ally instead of my enemy. I do not expect her to compromise because compromise, in her eyes, is just a slow surrender. I must figure out a way to allow the darkness to translate my teachings. My spirit must learn from the experiences that she attracts. Everyone chooses their own teachers. So, how do I convince her to have faith in what she cannot see?

Free Falling ∿

As my eyes open to witness a new day, my mind immediately begins to focus on the stresses in my life. I begin to fight with myself, shaking my head from left to right aggressively in pure disagreement with my mind. My spirit just wants to rest, to be in peace. I begin to argue with myself out loud. Though I was not fully healed, I began to use some of the techniques that I have learned. I spoke up and reminded myself to focus on what I want and not, on what I do not want. I feel like a crazy person but what else can I do? Physically, I do not have the resources to solve my problems. The resources exist, but for the life of me, I

31

cannot attract them. I cannot stop trying. I believe in my freedom, my freedom from debt, loneliness, hurt, and confusion to name a few. The more I chant out loud, "I AM FREE!" the more my mind focuses on the situations that have me shackled to this reality. I am no longer comfortable being a part of this reality and I want to get my mind right. I want my thoughts to line up with my spirit. The truth of the moment is that my emotions are lined up with my mind. Even though I am chanting at high vibrations, I can feel the anger building up inside of me. I can feel my heart being taken over by hurt and my mind is filled with confusion. I hear myself yelling and screaming. I can feel my legs kicking and my hands turning into fists. The room is spinning. Once again, I am losing control of myself.

I cannot focus. The only ideas that come to mind are the old ones and what good are they? They didn't work then and they will not work now. They might ease the pain temporarily, but it always comes back and here it is again.

The loneliness and financial problems have always traveled as a duo. Money can bring people together and it can split people apart. Here, in this dimension, they claim it makes the world go around. Right now, I am at a standstill. I do not idolize money; I understand it is necessary. I have a serious issue with the fact that a piece of paper is determining how I wake up in the morning.

Money should not have control over such a being. Here in this dimension, my spirit does not recognize its own divinity, its position in this universe. But this does not mean that I am any less divine, I just vibrate very low, a slowed version of my soul. Now, I am on a mission to vibrate faster, right here and right now. I cannot and will not continue to watch myself be tormented by my lack of knowledge. How did I lose sense of self? I must heal myself. I keep proclaiming my freedom out loud.

"I AM FREE! I AM FREE! I am worthy of my freedom simply because I exist."

It is dark. I am back in the tunnel. In the tunnel, I am free. Freedom is just understood here. How do I apply this knowledge and the understanding of it outside of the tunnel?

"You just be free."

I released a loud sigh as I received my instructions from the Great One. The door to the tunnel opens and I must go and be free. It is time for me to pass this test. I usually leap from the tunnel, but this time, I just stand on the edge. I stand there for a moment and witness the entire universe before me. It is peaceful. I tune in with the universe changing my molecular structure. I refuse to jump. Instead, I just fall freely into my next mission allowing my spirit to guide me. My spirit engulfs my lower vibrating self and nestles in comfortably. The moment I enter myself, I realized that in this world, I am not convinced that I have every answer to every question in my curious mind. I can change the course of our journey, if I would just trust myself.

Wake Up 〜

I rose out of bed. It was four hours after the craziness began. I feel better. I didn't remember going back to sleep but I am glad I did. I remember being handed a lottery ticket. I do not know who handed it to me and I do not remember the numbers. I just remember a voice saying, "Take this and see if it's a winner." I remember feeling a sense of relief when I received the ticket. At that moment, my life began to change. That voice spoke freedom into my life. All I have to do is be free. Right now, I know that I am a winner simply because I exist.

I look in the mirror right before I step into the shower. I see freedom and I claim it.

"I AM FREE."

Everything in my life that had me in bondage washes away in the shower. I step out pure, free, and healed. Now, I can continue with this journey.

Limbo 〜〜

Most are afraid of limbo. This is why I
choose it as my place of peace. Limbo is
simplistic, relaxing, and personal, a place where
nothing exist but your inner being. There are no
limitations, only opportunities.

The only wars that exist are of the mind. Some
attempt to free their minds and become trapped.
Every illusion that was created by the mind is
released, having no influence in limbo. The
only thing that exist in limbo is consciousness,
pure energy that allows you to travel faster than
sound and dwell amongst whomever, without
notice. Limbo is freedom. You can be all ages,

all beings, or all-knowing and all existence simultaneously. For most, this is too overwhelming. So, they escape limbo and exist in different galaxies as various creatures allowing the beings of their new experience to influence who they become. This is a transformation necessary to coexist in their new place. The Great One meets with everyone in the tunnel and instructs them about the life they are about to face. I am different from others because I frequent the tunnel, jumping from one galaxy to the next, planet to planet, experiencing the energy of various beings and absorbing their knowledge and wisdom.

There are still some beings in existence I have yet to encounter and gain knowledge from, but they cannot hide themselves or contain their vibrations for eternity. I know with patience, I will experience them as well. As I travel through limbo, I experience those that are trapped. They are not visible to me but I can feel their energy around me. Their souls are tormented by their own minds. They cannot make their way back to the tunnel.

A soul needs to continuously be born again but without the tunnel, this is impossible. The biggest threat to all existence is an unstable mind. Beings that enter into the tunnel must be ready to receive the instructions given by the Great One and carry them out. Many are called but few are ready to accept the true path. Still, we all exist together.

I have made a lot of connections throughout my existence. At times, I wonder if some are real or mere illusions of me. The Great One has taught me that everything is a reflection of self and this galaxy is a mirror image of the good and evil sides of me. The beings that I despise are just images of me that I despise. The loving and nurturing guides are simply my inner being taking care of itself. Limbo brings everything back to a state of understanding. There are no creatures to assist you and no beings to gain knowledge from, for any questions will be answered from within where the truth resides.

The Great One exists in infinite possibilities, as do I. I accept who I am which allows me to experience every single possibility that could cross one's mind, body, or soul. Each moment allows me to be the greatest or the weakest, to shine bright or become dark, to wonder in space or walk on the surface. My journeys are fulfilling the desires of my heart. My quests are successful because I do not allow failure to enter.

Free At Last? 〰

　　Life became interesting once I began to apply
the laws of the universe. Freedom has a price. I
started to notice the people, places, and
situations that began dissolving after I
proclaimed my freedom. That was all it took.
There is no need for conversations,
explanations, or painful goodbyes. The universe
will begin shifting things around on your behalf.
It is just that simple.

　　I wake up and claim my freedom.
Instantaneously, my situation begins to change.
Certain phone calls just stop ringing, certain
people just disappear, and peace is no longer a

destination I am seeking. I am peace. I am freedom. I am my own resource. Now that I have made the decision to accept and practice this new way of life, it is time to deal with these out of control personalities. In the process of being freed from the vampires, there still remains a spirit brewing inside of me that is extremely angry and violent. I can keep this spirit dormant for short periods of time. I thought I had control over them, but in actuality, I am just suppressing them. The longer I suppress Anger, the more violent she is. When a moment arises and she is released from her chains, all hell breaks loose. She does not discriminate. She will attack whomever, whenever, and usually, it is an innocent bystander who just happens to be in her presence at the wrong time.

They bother me deeply, some of the words that have spewed out of her mouth to the people that I love. The truth is she doesn't love anyone but herself, and she will fight when she feels threatened. The world has taught her this survival method and she is passing this process along to my off springs. It saddens me to see this energy transferred to such innocent souls, eating away at their light and introducing them to such a dark place. This energy generates from an incredibly deadly place known as fear. This anger derives from a place of not knowing what may or may not happen, not being in control. This is a place of confusion; I guess you could call it hell.

I cannot recall my first time visiting hell, but I was there so much that it became my home away from home. Though it isn't exactly where I want to be, it is necessary. In order to understand and appreciate the light, I have to understand and appreciate the dark. The challenge is learning from the dark and not getting caught up in it. I am caught. My life has become one big dark experience; it is my way of life. I find myself complaining, even in good situations. I sit on the couch for hours watching time go by not accomplishing anything. I get angry because I want to be free to move around, to smile, to be happy.

But in my mind and in my body, I know I do not deserve these things. I will just charge it to karma and accept my setbacks in life then find a way to put the blame of my miseries on other people. I do not know how to take responsibility for the shape that my soul is in. It is not my fault. Since it is not my fault, it is also not my job to pull myself up out of this mess. For years, I have waited. I have waited on a man to rescue me, you know, my knight in shining armor, my King, my soul mate. While waiting on this man I find an alternative love, money. I know, I can pay my way out of hell - but no matter what I do, I never have enough to foot the bill. My favorite attempt is to simply ignore hell, to pretend like this is not where I am right now, you know, smile when I am really hurting, dress up really nice, and become a whore for compliments or just hide in my shell, isolated from the world. I am out of control and far from reality. In the midst of my self-realization, I realize, I am not alone.

From Circles to Straight Lines, the Path to Greatness 〜〜

Being great requires knowing and embracing your weaknesses. The general idea would be to conquer or overcome such things within you, so that you can advance from great to greater and eventually be the greatest. It is easy to realize how you would like to be successful, but you cannot embrace this until you acknowledge and get control over what makes you weak. This is the real challenge. So ask yourself, "What is holding me back from greatness?"

This is a great question. What holds one back from greatness? One must take time out to acknowledge their truths. You must bring your

45

truth to the forefront and bear your own crosses. The easiest thing to do in this world is to cast an illusion. A majority of the beings that have graced my presence have lost their way. We wait for the moment that someone has a meltdown or has fallen face down to the earth before we offer our resources. Even then, all we do is offer meaningless combinations of weird words to cast an illusion of sympathy, or worse, empathy. We hoard our powers, our connections, and our insights about life in hopes of remaining on top. If my fellow men are hurting, I must appear to be strong. We cast this illusion of happiness in attempts to cover up our pain, our struggles, our fears, and our weaknesses. Deep down we are disgusted with ourselves, but why? To whom do we owe success? Too much energy has gone into being angry because we are currently focused on the things that should not matter, causing them to manifest and encompass our lives. The people, places, and situations that have caused disappointment, hurt, hardship, and confusion are the same people, places, and situations that we pour energy into in order to attract our universe. Now it is here and it seems so simple, right? Does it make you weak or does it make you great?

You have to decide for yourself. If it makes you weak, dig deeper to understand why and how it makes you weak, being completely honest. In order to deal with your weakness you must embrace it and bring light to it. At this moment, prepare to take your power back. You have two options:

Option one is to remain attached to the weakness. Be aware, with every breath you take in this world, your weaknesses will follow you and forever be a part of you. Your weaknesses will haunt you for as long as your energy exists. It will pass on to your off-springs as well as theirs. They are curses designed to keep you in the dark. These curses will hold you deep within the matrix, to keep you from fulfilling your greatness. Your weaknesses will create generations of failures. Is this the legacy you want to continue in this universe?

Option two is for you to detach from your weaknesses and allow them to dissolve. Allow your weaknesses to fizzle and evaporate into the atmosphere, then return to you a new energy that is productive and true. Once you master this technique, greatness will surface on its own. Your greatness is not something that requires years of education or strenuous efforts. Your greatness exists simply because you exist. You have not been created to achieve anything less than greatness. You do not have to be worthy, you do not have to deserve it, you do not have to earn it, and it cannot be given to you. Greatness is the very essence of your soul. If you cannot see this, do not know this, cannot understand this, then of course you do not believe. Think about it...you may have attributed your lack of greatness to people, your environment, or missed opportunities in life, but the truth is you lack vision.

You have never seen or touched greatness because your circle is weak. A circle is a continuous 360 degrees. Once you have made it completely around the circle your end becomes your beginning. The truth is, there is never an ending to your circle of madness, confusion, or fear. Nothing will change. There will never be a new cycle until you change circles. You cannot achieve infinite greatness without new cycles. Now that you know this, apply it and you will understand. Every cycle is necessary in order to gain new knowledge and understanding so that you may be great and wise.

Wisdom is proof that one is great. In order for these energies to be set in motion, one must believe. You have to believe that greatness exists and is attainable at all times. The cycle of attaching and detaching is going to happen whether you choose to control it or allow it to control you. Either way, you are making a decision whether it is conscious or not. Today and every day that follows, you must consciously choose to detach from your curses. It may hurt but the pain will dissolve. It may seem hard but it will get easier. You may feel vulnerable but if you do, smile and take another step forward.

Whatever you think will be on the other side of that footstep will be your reality and the more steps you take in faith, in the midst of being vulnerable, the greater you will become. This road is less traveled but with faith, you will never have to travel this road alone. Your circle will become a straight line. Being vulnerable is your starting point and greatness is your destination. It is time to turn your circles into straight lines. Then, you can walk in greatness and declare, "I am more than a conqueror. I am the greatest me of all time!"

Let Your Guard Down 〰

    My greatness depends on my ability or inability to be honest with myself. I can continue to create new illusions to mask the truth or I can stare my truth straight in the eye and listen. I know it is time for me and my truth to have a conversation. Why am I so nervous? I feel like I am getting ready to go on a blind date. I am excited and terrified all at the same time. What if Truth doesn't look anything like she sounds? Her voice is intimidating, yet protective. Her words are not intended to make me feel any particular emotions; Truths' only job is to set me free. For every time I turned a deaf ear to her, I remained trapped in a world of confusion, lies, and fear. I am the prisoner and the guard of the miseries I created. It is challenging to be freed from such chaos and the silly thing is I hold the key to my own cell.

As a prisoner I confess my innocence daily but the guard is not listening. The guard will not allow me to be free. She isn't even considering unlocking this cell. I explain my story to her again and again. I yell, kick, and scream trying to show her that I do not deserve to be mistreated and her only response is,

"That doesn't sound like the truth to me."

Doesn't sound like the truth? But, I don't deserve to be bound to this life that I am experiencing at this moment. I want out of this moment! I want these chains to be taken off of my soul. I want to choose when I can come and go, rise, rest, and the company that I keep. I have the right to be whomever I choose. The guard is reading my thoughts, so she responds, "Indeed you have the right to be whomever you choose but why is it necessary to choose?

Your focus should not be on transforming into this or that for the sake of the moment. The focus should be on being you. In doing so, the moment will flow with you, and together, you will be successful."

These words pierce me like a double-edged sword. I recognize the voice. It is her, my long lost love. I just heard my truth. It is time to face my demons. It is time to change circles. Truth just smacked me in the face, revealing a weakness to me, control. I am in this cage having this moment because of my desire to control everything.

"Just lose control and your freedom awaits you..."

That sounds so easy and yet, I cannot grasp the idea at this moment. It sounds as if my freedom is only seconds away from manifesting itself and my mind is focused on the "what ifs." What if this door opens and I cannot handle freedom? Leaving this cell does not free me from this prison.

It just moves me from a small cage to a larger one. The guard places the key in the lock and turns it. The door creeps open and she walks away. I begin to think about my current situation. Now that the door is unlocked, this cage doesn't seem that bad. My responsibilities are very minimal. All my basic needs are taken care of and it is small but easy to manage. What will happen if I step outside of this door? I don't know what is out there. So many moments I have spent right here in this cage, by myself, begging the guard to let me out. My protests are for my freedom. As I stand here contemplating stepping outside of this box, Truth begins to whisper in my ear.

"Do not attempt to control this moment; allow this moment to control you. Stop analyzing the situation and make a move. You are either attached to this moment or you are detaching from it. Understand this: This moment will continue no matter what you decide. You will either be stuck in the moment or flowing with it. The choice is yours."

54

I stand here unsure of myself. I think I want something different but I am not sure I am ready for change. Hours pass and a breeze from the other side of the door brushes across my face. It feels so good. Is this what freedom feels like; a cool breeze massaging my skin? I do not know a life without the guard telling me what to do and when to do it. I just sit here unable to make the decision to accept or deny freedom. All this time, I have despised the guard; I hate what she represents. Every chance I have,

I let her know how much I despise her and this prison. I cannot help but cry. I thought the guard was my oppressor, the stumbling block that stands in between me and my freedom. But the guard is just an illusion, my scapegoat. At this moment, I am face to face with the truth and the truth is, my freedom has never been taken away from me. I handed it over and now I have the chance to take it back. Here I stand with my eyes closed and my ears covered, ignoring the truth. I cannot believe I let my guard down. No pun intended.

Con – fa – dense 〜〜

The key to freedom is realizing that you are
free. Freedom is one hundred percent mental.
The challenge is convincing your mind of this
lifestyle. In doing so, one will remain free from
the bondage of bills and others. If I could fight
myself right now, I would. I would punch me in
the face, kick me in the ribs, bite my shoulder,
and snatch a hand full of hair. I love sleep too
much to allow my financial worries to disrupt
my moment of peace, but dammit, at this
moment, I am one hundred percent in the flesh
and I hate the way it feels.

I just want to raise the window and scream
fuckkkkkkkkk - but that wouldn't change

anything but the neighbors' perception. I need
to face my weaknesses head-on. Every day, I
have managed to be sane, more or less, to not
show how really fucked-up I feel inside. I got
lazy. There, I said it. I sat around watching time
pass just thinking how much I have helped
others and I was confident that the time would
come for others to help me. This could very
well be the truth but I am guessing it is not the
people that I have in my mind. I have come to a
crossroad, one path is wide and consumed with
familiar faces and the other path is narrow and
lonely. The longer I stay in this environment,
the longer I am going to dwell in what has
become my hell.

I need a solution. Every day, I remind the
Universe that I will always have what I need.
By my waking hour, I need the solution to my
current sleeping disorder. I am claiming my
peace and I believe in my peace. I guess, this is
good night and sweet dreams.

I Am You ∿

What do you do when you hit rock bottom?
Remember that you are God.

I am more than a conqueror but I still need to
conquer all of my weaknesses. I have spent a
majority of my life preying on the weak,
keeping the weak close, making sure I know and
understand all of their problems and attempt to
solve every last one of them. It makes me feel
superior. It gives me power. How did I end up
in this situation? Why am I reflecting over my
life? Why am I disgusted with who I see in the
mirror? The answer is simple, because I am
weak. For every weak person I took in, I

became that person. Just like them, every
problem I had, I ran. Low and behold, I finally
reached the point where I could not help myself.
Like them, I began to search outside sources. I
found the people I helped were not interested in
helping me. They lacked the resources and
desire to complete such a task. I was offered
complaints, lies, and excuses. They didn't have
a direction for me, other than, the path they were
travelling. I could not believe my dilemma.
The same world that looked in my face then
proclaimed their love for me, is the same world
that has turned its back to me. I am them. I too,
am looking for somebody great to pull me out of
this place of need. I have crossed the paths of
imitators. They led me down paths of
destruction. Now, I have lost everything. I lost
my peace, my happiness, my joy, my respect,
my integrity, and my identity. I am riding on
grace and even that seems to be coming to an
end. For six years, I have watched everything
that I have worked hard for dissolve. I watched
it happen resting in a state of denial. I still
proclaimed my greatness.

The little bit of dignity I had tucked away, was taken from me and I just sat there and watched it happen.

So now, I am a prisoner. I have nowhere to go and nothing to do. I wait to be told what happens next. I have forfeited control over my life. Even my ego has left me, my best friend in the entire world. I cannot pretend any longer that I am on top of this world. I have become one of them. I accept that I am weak. The hunter is now being hunted. Instead of running or fighting, I just stand here out in the open, naked and exposed, waiting to be saved. Who will find me first, my oppressor or my savior? What has happened to my pride? Where did I place my integrity? I lost my faith and I no longer believe in miracles. Where is God? Better yet, who is God? I do not know if it is the end days for the entire world, but I know I am facing my last and evil days.

I closed my eyes so I could no longer see the world. As soon as my lids shut, all signs of light disappear and I am alone in the dark. "Hello? Is there anyone here? If there is, please say something..."

I am scared. Anxiety is building up and fear is taking over. I feel my hands pulling at my hair. I feel my mouth moving as if I am screaming but there is no sound. I hear a different voice but not through my ears. I hear a whisper, a soft and calm whisper, and it spoke to me. "I am here." I open my eyes to see the same scene that I had just shut out, so I yell... "WHO IS HERE?"

Silence follows my voice and no one appears. I begin to walk toward what sounds like a body of water. The sound is so calm and refreshing. I am sure my mind is playing tricks on me. The whisper is still echoing in my head and words are somehow resonating from somewhere other than my mouth. As I continue walking, I can only focus on the three words, I am here. I am here. I do not know where here is, technically. I am unable to describe my surroundings. I can hear my environment but I lack vision.

61

Still, I journey towards what sounds like water. I continued with my journey to nowhere, alone. I silence my thoughts in case the whisper returns. If I accept I am here, in this unknown place, I obtained this information by posing a question. I try my luck and ask another one, "Why am I here?"

I remain silent, anticipating a response. I stop walking and focus on listening. I watch the light fade into the dark as my eyes seal themselves shut. In addition to the darkness, there is now complete silence. I can no longer hear the sounds of water. I am scared but I stand still. I can feel a response coming. So, I wait. At this point, the concept of time escapes me, but it feels like days have passed and still, I patiently wait for a response. Though I cannot hear myself, I decide to ask the question again, out loud,

"Why am I here?"

As soon as the last syllable vibrates off my tongue, I feel a great wind dance across my body.

Wind has never felt like this. It is going straight through me. As it passes, I can feel it transforming me. My thoughts shift from my head to my heart and my heart begins to sing. The melodies are so touching and beautiful; I can feel tears flowing down my face. Even though I cannot hear, I know in my heart that the tears sound like that body of water I was walking towards just moments ago. This experience is overwhelming. I am so taken that I can no longer feel my legs and gravity is snatched from underneath me. I fall flat on my face - lying prostrate in this place simply known as here. My heart stopped singing and spoke to me, "You are here, because this is where I need you to be."

Suddenly, I am no longer confused, or afraid, or alone. This has to be my savior. This must be the one who is going to turn things around for me. This has to be my saving grace; this is God. I try to move my lips, so that I can ask one final question. I cannot see. I cannot hear. But, I do have a voice. I choose to speak. I know exactly what I want to ask and then, I realize I cannot move my lips.

I feel trapped inside of myself but strangely I am comfortable. There is no such thing as an outside world at this moment. I am comfortable in my own skin. I am surprisingly calm and at peace with myself. I am enjoying being alone with me. From the outside looking in, I have lost the ability to commune with the world but I have gained the ability to commune with myself. I cannot express myself through my voice or my mind. I can only express what comes from my heart. I asked my final question straight from my heart, "Are you God?"

What feels like hours pass and then I ask again, "Are you God?" As I sit, waiting patiently on a response, my darkness begins to shed light. The experience is amazing - no words can describe. I see every color of the spectrum. I watch the colors interact and intertwine, full of energy displaying endless combinations of pure beauty. I am in awe. My heart is full and I am sure that tears are streaming down my face, but I can no longer feel anything outside of myself.

It is electrifying like the energy produced when a human egg is fertilized and creation begins. Instantly, I can feel again, but the only thing that I can feel is the pumping of my heart. Now, I am able to hear, but I can only hear the thumping of my heart and almost immediately my vision returns - I can see my heart throbbing and radiating life. I know that I am in the presence of God. I know this is God. I am experiencing him right now, right here, in this place where I need to be. This place known as here is where the answer to my final question is revealed. The answer is simple and it speaks directly to my heart, "I am you."

Everything is silent and black. I feel a tug at my hand and I can hear voices. As my eyes slowly open, I see machines, I see people, and I hear cries as well as celebration. A voice cries out, "Thank you God for bringing her back. Thank you for saving her."

I know I just experienced God. I was in the wilderness, alone, waiting to be saved and I was. I saved myself.

As I ponder the miracle I just witnessed, I hear a voice explaining how stressed I was and that I had suffered from a heart attack. I blacked out and my heart stopped. She went on to say that God brought me back. God saved me. I was back, back on my path to greatness. Of course, God brought me back to life because I am God. God is me and I am God. Now that I am fully aware of who I am, I will continue through this world in the spirit. I will walk on water, overcome my enemies, and spread the good news.

I have already been crucified and left for dead. Today, I rise with all power to conquer the world. This is simply one version of the story; this is my story which makes it your story when we agree that I am you, and then you too shall be saved, "For my grace is sufficient for you, for my strength is made perfect in weakness."
(2 Corinthians 12:9, The Holy Bible)

Self-Centered 〰

As you witness yourself through interactions
with others, you will become one with yourself.
Embrace criticism with a passion. The more
your flaws are drawn to the surface, the easier it
will be to master them. Only a fool denies his
dark side. Learn to use your flaws against the
people who try to conquer you. You are all
things, so you will experience everything. This
will cause confusion in the physical realm but
will separate the real from the fake. Who shall
be so bold to be the first to speak out and say, "I
am centered?" Who shall be so carefree to
smile and take pride in knowing that he is not
perfect? It is easy to diagnose the illnesses of

another but who is great enough to heal himself? The only remedy is self- healing through self-realization. One cannot heal another being from a dis-ease that he has never experienced. If one should be so foolish to attempt such a task, dis-ease will enter the life of the inexperienced and begin to teach a lesson. The reality is you want this experience and the universe will provide you with one. What you hate, you will attract. The same principal applies to love. What you attract and experience, are direct results of what you simultaneously love and hate.

Now that I am aware of this truth, I can protect myself. I strive to vibrate high at all times. I know this is being achieved when I experience peace that surpasses all understanding. The right now is determined by me. I choose to laugh or cry. I choose to listen or speak. I choose to be with or without. I choose to own my destiny. I am self-centered. Self, meaning I am aware of who I am from every possible perspective, whether it be a dark experience or light. Centered, meaning balance

68

has been maintained as I savor each moment of all my experiences. Never am I more in darkness than in light. I just am.

I do not value the opinions of others. I know myself to well to believe in such judgments. The Great One will only allow others to see a being that is aware of itself. It is arrogant to think that anyone would know something about another before they know themselves. It is a fool who thinks he possesses this wisdom. If your focus and energy are directed toward revealing someone else to themselves then you are concluding they are lost. The truth is you are experiencing your own soul reflected from the one you are judging. In essence, you are seeing yourself. You are the one that is lost and you prove it by looking outside of yourself and judging what you see. How can you categorize someone else's essence if you have not experienced it yourself? You can only identify the things in others that you possess. There are many that lack an understanding and this too is by choice. I can only harness the energy of qualities that will carry on my destiny to be centered.

Through it all, my soul remains innocent and flawless. It is my body going through the motions reflecting the energy that occupies my space. How you see me and what you see in me, is a reflection of what you are experiencing. If you see my soul, then no flaws exist. If it is my mind, then my thoughts are your thoughts. But, if the experience is strictly physical, then you are vibrating too low to understand. This experience is yours and not mine, for I do not exist in a world that is not aware of self and unbalanced. Greatness does not experience lowliness nor do the strong understand the ways of the weak. We know of no such world.

Unbalanced: Ego Vs. Love 〜〜

I had everything I thought I wanted and the
feeling lasted for a few days. Now, I miss him,
his scent, his tone, and his thoughts. Is this what
it feels like to not know? I wonder if the one
who told me he loved me yesterday is thinking
about me today. My ego scared away my
happiness. We all have flaws but the more you
handle, the closer you are to experiencing
eternal love. This type of love will not allow
any situation to come between you; a union that
understands the strength of the love that is

shared. A love so great that mountains move on command, raging waves of the ocean simmer in its presence, and the earth stills on its axis. This love is respected by all forms of creation. A love which produces more love and inspires the existence of something new, never experienced. This is the type of love I am capable of giving and feigning to receive.

My ego is small enough now, that I can acknowledge and accept my wrong doings then do what is necessary to make them right again. But when I am right, my ego is HUGE and my pride shows through my chest. I will fight to the point that I lose what I love to prove I am right; then, being right isn't important anymore. Being right and being humble go hand in hand. Being understood is a gift from the heavens. There is no right or wrong in understanding. There is just peace, prosperity, and love. We often have mistaken our need for being understood with our ego's need to be right. I just want to be understood. I need him to understand that love scares me. Love has disappointed me. Love has seduced me. Love has made me act out of impulse because it felt right. Even though I don't understand love, it feels right.

Again, I have mistaken the need to be right, with the need to be understood, and the truth is, I love so that I can be understood. Love is how I understand him but I am not sure if he understands me.

I thought I was taking the pain away. But, today I feel like I am causing pain. I know he doesn't trust me but I don't understand why. My ego will not allow me to ask him even though I know it is the missing piece of the puzzle. Complications, confusion, and wasted time this is now our focus instead of love, peace, and prosperity. I miss him. What happened? Will we use our gift of forever just to figure out who commanded the cease and desist between us or will we let yesterday vanish and start from today?

Does yesterday matter if our love is true? Our love should be able to endure anything, if it is true love...

I guess this is the test and it is simple, the imagination versus the spirit. If he thinks it, then it is his truth and I am not sure what our love will be able to withstand. My heart aches because it knows it has been true - though hesitant; it has been true. I guess only time will tell.

Finding Confidence 〜〜

I am in search of my greatest ally within me
and her name is Confidence. She is not just
anyone. She is the greatest support of all, "My
Confidence." How did I manage to separate
myself from her? Did I misplace her or worse,
did I allow someone or something to snatch her
from me? Perhaps, she just left.

So many attempts at success in this
dimension resulting in so many failures. But
even through the rough times and
disappointments, she was always there to pick
me up and carry me to the next phase of life.

She always wipes my tears and paints a smile on my face. She makes me laugh in the face of rejection then allows me to pinch a little off her and share her with a friend in need.

I have searched high and low for her, well maybe not. The truth is, I have isolated myself from this world thinking, "If I just stay put, she will find her way back to me." I sit here and I wait. In the midst of my waiting, I receive a visit from a woman that goes by the name, Patience. Her presence is comforting and she promises she will continue to check on me. She offers to help me look for Confidence. Her willingness to help me search for my dear friend is highly appreciated but every time I am ready to go out into this world and begin my hunt for Confidence, she is never ready. She explains that she has work to do and I explain to her that I do not have time to work on anything else. What could be more important than finding Confidence right now?

Patience began to explain her work to me, "The task before us consists of more than just running out into this world and turning over every rock, then looking behind every tree. Are you prepared for what lies underneath the first rock? I can guarantee without your Confidence you will not be able to handle it."

I held my head in shame. She is right. There isn't much that I can do without Confidence.

"Come here and have a meal with me," Patience insist. I sit peacefully at the table hungry for whatever Patience has to offer. She showed up at the right time because I am utterly lost with my Confidence missing and need a true friend.

"When a Tortoise sets out on a journey whether it is long or short, easy or difficult, for pleasure or necessity, he always takes his time. His shell represents his confidence; a true friend that he will never go about life without. The Tortoise can swim, walk, float, dig, run, or just be still. One of the reasons the Tortoise has maintained its existence in this world for so many ages is simple.

It has established a lifelong relationship with me, Patience. At times, the Tortoise faces situations without confidence. It crawls into its shell and there I am working, until his confidence returns and his journey continues."

I cannot believe what I am hearing. Without Patience, I may never have Confidence again. I ask her,

"How long is it going to take before I can have Confidence back? As she continues to work, she leans in and whispers, "Have Patience my friend."

I work with Patience day in and day out. Sometimes the work is especially challenging and I need to take a break. Patience never stops working but she never complains when I run out on her. Other days I feel great and begin my work before Patience even arrives. When she does show up, she just joins right in. I notice that my momentum shifts when she enters my space. I begin to match hers and that frustrates me. I don't complain out loud. I just mumble to myself. On one of my frustrating days in the middle of my mumble, Patience comes to a halt.

"What are you mumbling?"

I am surprised by her question and somewhat embarrassed.

"You do not have to tell me now. I can wait."

We continue our work and I want to share with her my thoughts. I want to open up to her and explain, there are days I hate spending time working with Patience because she always takes forever. The days I begin without Patience, time flies by and I focus on finishing work so I can go search for Confidence, like we agreed. With Patience in my life, my momentum slows down. Every day, I want to say, "The hell with Patience," then go off on my own to find Confidence, but instead I mumble, "Let Patience do her perfect work. Let Patience do her perfect work," over and over again. Instead of answering her question, I ask her one...

"What are we working on anyway and how is it going to help me find Confidence? Some days we dig. Some days we walk. Other days we run. We may eat and sometimes we just sit."

She smiles, keeps working and responds,

"Every day, I work for you and if you think back to right before you lost your precious Confidence, you lost me. So, if you will just continue to work with Patience, then I am sure that we will not need to go searching for your Confidence. I do not believe she left. You just don't recognize her now. The days I show up and you are already working, you are not working alone.

You are digging and walking and running with Confidence. But until you sit still and reflect on your work, you will never recognize her. What you are failing to realize is your Confidence was never lost...she evolved into a new Confidence so she may guide you through new experiences. But, you are only focused on getting the work finished for the sake of completing a task instead of doing the work in order to move forward. At times, moving forward consists of being still so that your Confidence can grow. My work is perfect and necessary for your Confidence to exist and evolve.

The instant the last word exited her mouth, my new Confidence stood before me. She is so amazing.

Now, I have the Patience I need to go along with my new Confidence. We are all co-existing and I have the necessary resources to move forward in this new world. I am not sure what lies ahead but I have the Patience and the Confidence to continue on my journey.

The lifetime you experience in this dimension is not about what you deserve. It is simply a manifestation of the energies that you attract. Greatness will follow you throughout your many life experiences if you choose but so can defeat. Choose wisely, so that your soul will be satisfied.

Free to Be 〰

I pulled myself from under the covers and headed toward the bathroom. As I brush my teeth I can see and feel my aura glowing. I feel as light as a feather floating around my house. The person I see in the mirror is amazing, inspiring, and sexy. I cannot stop staring at this woman reflecting from the mirror to my eyes and back to the mirror.

Mesmerized by the soul reflected, I have to ask, "Who are you?"

"I am you..."

The response is startling, yet refreshing. "If you are me, then who am I?"

"I am free..."

"Free to be what?"

"Free to be..."
The response is so broad. I have a pretty decent understanding of the word free but it is something about the way I said it to myself, that has me confused.

Mental Progression 〜

Sometimes the hardest thing to do is keep going. It separates the winners from the losers. If at some point I stop, I always know that I can start again. Losing is a state of mind; it is acknowledging the fact that something I had is gone. Winning is a state of spirit; it is acknowledging the fact that I will always have what I need and I will always get what I want. I am abundant; therefore, whatever is lost is necessary to make room for what I desire. My energy is powerful yet sacred. Whatever I enforce is destined for greatness simply because I Am. Remember, the end is the beginning. A

new season cannot start until the current one
ends. Appreciate your gains and your losses.

Soul Mates 〰〰

The desire to be with my soul mate consumes
my heart causing my mind to produce
overwhelming thoughts of love. I am longing
for his energy like a mother in labor patiently
waiting to lay eyes on this spirit that she has
connected with for what feels like forever. I
paint pictures in my mind of what he looks like
in the flesh and I hope that he fits the description
but I cannot dwell on what he looks like
physically. I have to exercise patience and
confidence so I do not look right past him when
he presents himself. Nothing can satisfy this
urge but his presence. His demeanor is beyond

that of a King. He is an amazing being to whom the utmost respect is given. The power he has established during his tenure, tips the scales in comparison to those around him. His gracefulness balances his ego allowing him to be humble, especially, in the company of those less fortunate. He is loved by many, but only desires one, me, the being known to this universe as, The Vision. All of his focus is on The Vision which sparks my existence to manifest. Every essence of female energy causing him to take notice resonates within me.

If he thinks it and it makes him smile, then I am a collection of his thoughts manifested. I exist in this realm because he called me down from the heavens so that he may experience pleasure in its purest form. I am here because he will not exist in this universe without me, nor will I.

I saw him once outside my dreams. I was in the presence of nineteen thousand other souls who screamed and longed for him. He sang to me.

Our spirits rose above the crowd and danced in Atlanta, Georgia, on a cloudy Friday evening in the beloved month of September, his hair was blonde and his skin the color of Brazilian coffee beans. I was in my natural form, hair extending high from my crown like a million little antennas receiving every sensual instruction, inebriated from the finest grapes known to man. My skin was shining like I had just received Gods glory and my shirt announced that the water bearer, also known as The Vision, was in attendance. His performance was genuine. He was home and sitting on his thrown. I closed my eyes and took in all of his energy and when I opened them, we made the world disappear again.

I stood center stage in front of an infinite amount of energy. The screams and yells went silent. It was not a normal silence known to this planet. It resembled the silence experienced in space. I could hear the beat of my heart and the pulsating of my veins but they made it difficult to locate him because his heartbeat matched mine. I could feel his presence.

I could see the nineteen thousand souls but they couldn't see me. The darkness covered me from head to toe draping my body like a spirit of protection.

He told me that the show would start when I started glowing. It was my divine right. He told me the energy I was going to experience on this night was going to set the stage on fire and when the windows to my soul open, the world would change. The funny thing is he inherited the Earth and if he wanted me to have it, he could just hand it to me but that was not his vision. Being given the world is a gift indeed, but being able to take the world, is a skill. It was God knowledge and I had to learn how to be a Goddess outside of the heavens. Our mission is not limited to this world. We are more than conquerors.

I began to embrace the darkness, our place of peace. I could feel my soul glowing. Suddenly, I was overtaken by the light. The light shined so bright. This energy was bigger than bliss and my soul engulfed it like a baby taking its mothers breast and enjoying the elixir of life. The energy was infinite, continuously building around me as well as inside of me. I could feel him inside of me. I was glowing and it felt like fire trapped in my bones. Gravity didn't exist. Darkness didn't exist. The only thing that existed was the light and then it happened. Sound existed again.

As I opened the windows to my soul, I find myself back in Atlanta, sitting on the lawn, surrounded by nineteen thousand screaming souls. I smile because he took time to cater to me. I no longer care that he is rocking a blonde wig and wearing a black parachute style jumpsuit. I recognize him for who he is, at least who he is to me, my soul mate. We have just shared a cosmic kiss and this world is ours for the taking. For, this is the first time that I tasted victory.

Thick Out Here 〜〜

One hundred and sixty-six pounds is what the scale registered as I stood there witnessing how low I was vibrating based on how dense this scale is telling me my flesh is...I am thick.

For some weeks now, okay months, my one hundred and forty-seven pound version of me has been taking on the challenge of dealing with this new version of her. She is wild; she thinks that we are two separate beings. She stays frustrated because she keeps trying to get me into her clothes and we manage to get them on but not comfortably. I take the blame for her feelings. It makes me sad because she is sad. I wish she could just see my perspective. This is the only way I can exist, if she loses the weight she loses me. I want her to stop being so selfish and let me have my moment. This is my experience and she needs to quit feeling sorry for herself. Hell, I'm good! I try to take her shopping but she never wants to go. She always says, "I am not going shopping until I lose this weight!" I never stay long. This is about my fifth time visiting and three of those visits were for the kids. This is only the second time I have been here and not had a huge belly to go along with it. Can I have my moment please? Is that too much to ask?

I want this to be a rock star experience. I want the opportunity to embrace and celebrate. Let's enjoy the change. At least, we have an ass and hips right now. She always complains about not having those attributes but they can only exist if I do.

Limit the jogging pants and huge sweat shirts. Let's dress these curves up! When you look at us in the mirror stop calling me fat!

Tell me that I am sexy. I love hearing it just as much as you do. It is still our time to shine. I swear you are the only person I know that can't stand me.

I never know how long she is going to keep me around, I plan on enjoying every moment possible. I promise her the world will love us but she has to love us first.

No Pain – No Gain 〰

I show a lot of compassion toward others but never look for that same compassion in return. Or, do I?

Is this why I feel heartless at the moment? I understand everyone else's pain and situations but have neglected to understand my own. I am capable of being hurt. I am just not capable of feeling the pain.

This weed has me numb to it all. I just take a toke and then go along with the ride. Now that I have set the pipe down, I can feel the pain from these bruises to my body, my ego, and my soul. I could always see them. I just never allowed myself to feel them. All the pain hasn't hit me yet. I guess that's God's grace being bestowed on me. But, I know the pain at some point will come crashing down on my world.

While I have momentum, I am trying to tend to one bruise at a time healing myself. I have to choose wisely. My ego has probably been bruised the worst but the treatment to heal it is the easiest. Do I start with easy and end with hard? My soul has taken the biggest hit and I am sure I will need a medically induced coma to begin my healing. Never-never land is the destination for the necessary treatment to heal my soul. Which one gets priority, my ego or my soul?

Corporate Slave 〜〜

That alarm clock sounded today and I said,
"You know what? No more working for me, no
more slaving for master, no more cussing, and
no more fussing."

I dressed in all black as if I had a funeral to
attend. Who was dead? That corporate chick,
the one that's chasing the paper instead of letting
the paper chase her is dead. I walked into that
office so classy today but no good mornings and
no goodbyes because these are her co-workers.
I don't know them nor do they know me. I
gently lay down her badge and keys and didn't

bother to leave a separation notice - just "notice"
that she doesn't work here anymore - she's dead,
I buried her ass about an hour ago.

May She Rest in Peace? 〰

Will she rest in peace? Today, we say goodbye
to our dear friend Anger. Her entire existence
was birthed through Chaos. Chaos married a
fine man named Anguish. Chaos came from a
bloodline of Pain and Anguish is some kin to
Frustration. This union birthed a beautiful baby
named Anger.

Anger lived a life filled with violence and
turmoil. No one would come close to her
because they could not deal with her Frustration,
Pain, Anguish, and Chaos. This hurt Anger
dearly. Anger tried her best to isolate herself
from this world so that she would not cause

discomfort to anyone else. She figured the only way she could put an end to it all was to be alone. Anger would go to the library and read books that were written about her. She found one that suggested there was a way to stay in control. She read for days and the book suggested that she needed to find Peace. She had never heard of this person but the book made Peace sound like the best person in the world. So, Anger set out on a mission to find Peace.

Anger searched high and low for her beloved Peace. He was not familiar to anyone Anger knew. In the midst of her journey, Anger grew tired of searching for Peace. She past a cemetery on her way home and noticed that all the tombstones read the same, "May she rest in peace." Anger figured the only way to find Peace was through death. She went home, she found some poison, she drank it, and she lay on her bed. She left a note for her parents that simply read, "I am resting in Peace."

Chaos and Anguish found their daughter resting. They planned her funeral and buried her. A man came to the funeral that was unfamiliar to Chaos and Anguish. He asked to speak and they allowed him. They had never known Anger to have friends so they were curious as to whom this strange man was and what he had to say about Anger.

"Today we bury our sister Anger. We keep her locked up inside the chambers of our hearts and through her I am able to exist. Many of you do not recognize me but I am a friend of the family. I am the Peace that Anger has searched for all of her existence."

Chaos began to cry because she knew her secret was about to be revealed.

"Anger is my twin; we were separated at birth because our mother, Chaos, could not exist with the both of us in her presence. How could Chaos be herself in the midst of Peace? How could my father Anguish live up to his name amongst Peace? How could Anger and Peace be raised together without one influencing the other to be something they are not? I cannot judge you mother for giving me away at birth but Anger was only searching for her other half all of these years. No one ever thought that anything good would come from Anger but in her misery, she found me. She rests and abides in me and today my sister experiences me, Peace. Now we lay her to rest. Anger we honor you."

Anguish could not believe what he was hearing. But he was a gentle man and hugged his wife Chaos; then they wept.

Caterpillars & Butterflies ∿

The wings of a caterpillar are hidden deep
within. Though the world cannot see them,
there is a universal understanding that they exist.
When the time is right the caterpillar will sleep,
shutting itself out from all existence, and when
it raises itself from the dead, it will be a new
creature with a new mind, a new mission, a new
name, and a renewed spirit, ready to experience
the same world from a new point of view.

I know I want to be the butterfly but I have yet
to accept the fact that first I must be the
caterpillar. Why is it challenging to appreciate
the things about me that make me who I am in

this caterpillar stage? The caterpillar appears to be exceptionally balanced, no one part greater than the other, all working together for the greater good of becoming the butterfly. Am I aware of the beauty that is right before me or do I just live for the future when I sprout wings and fly? As exciting as it may seem, I must allow the future to surface in its rightful season so the experience will be new to me and not borrowed from those who have already transitioned into butterflies. I cannot get so caught up in what is ahead that I forget to savor the moment known as right now. I have to crawl before I fly and when I do fly, I will pay homage to those that crawled before me and those that continue to crawl.

Cosmic Orgasm 〜〜

I lost him. Clearly our missions have changed.
He has a journey that does not include me. I
still have a lot to discover on my own, as does
he.

This place is familiar. I nestled right into this
new experience. This palace is amazing and the
aroma is mind boggling. Every facet of my
existence is in pure awe, a new bliss. Who is
the one behind this experience? I want to share
this lovely heaven with the soul that is
responsible for this atmosphere.

The Great I Am is satisfied; this is as close to home as it gets. A being of such beauty, elegance, and grace is forever humbling to the Master of this place. This palace is nowhere near fit for a King or a Queen. It must be of the Gods and Goddesses. This is the seventh dimension. It has to be. My soul is as light as a feather. My eyes reflect the beauty of this glorious experience at its core causing a connection greater than the cosmos. This is not a world. This one raw experience is vibrating so fast that every amazing interaction prior causes my crown to vibrate down to my root. As I seduce myself into a frequency so high every galaxy is evolving, a thought comes to a new beginning because here in this dimension, nothing ever ends...

I woke up this morning with a tingle running up my spine. I am different, I am a new creature and I feel amazing. I am ready for the mirror, ready to reflect on my yesterday, today, and tomorrow, right now. I am caught in the moment. The shower is running hot. The steam gives the bathroom a heavenly presence.

I face the mirror, naked down to my soul, and I begin to tell myself who I am... "I am free, I am confident, I am beautiful, I am great, I am patient, I am abundant, and I am at peace with myself."

The more I tell myself who I am, the lighter my load feels. Nothing is heavy about today. I am so high on life I know anything is possible. Today, I vibrate possibilities. Not only will I have what I want, I will have it in abundance.

I crack a smile because today I believe my truth. I hear my truth loud and clear and she doesn't have any lies to tell.

Sleeping Naked 〜〜

The only thing I wear in his presence is my sensual aura. Every experience with him is new. I walk into his presence with thoughts of being touched by him. I use his fingers as a paintbrush transforming me into a priceless work of art inspired by him.

On our last encounter he sculpted me into a beautiful masterpiece. His vibrations turned my coils into silky tresses, my almond eyes into a seductive glimpse of heaven, my lips became the color of the finest wine, and my hips move like the ocean performing a sexual mantra on a clear night with the moon full.

He witnesses me. If he thinks it, I become it.
As he abides in me, I abide in him. Naked, we
sleep as one.

Who Are You? 〰

You spend most of your days judging yourself instead of being yourself. BE FREE!

If heaven and hell were not the final options for life after death, who would you really be? That is the person I want to know, the real you. I want to know this simply because you exist.

Maybe your frowns and disappointments stem from the belief that if you die right now, based on the life you lived thus far, you will not make it into heaven. You are so afraid of spending eternity in hell that you focus on evil day in and day out.

How can we spend forever in a place that never crosses our minds? Heaven sounds like a wonderful place to spend eternity but do you feel like you deserve to spend infinity in a place that is fit for angels and Gods? This life is not about what you deserve.

You have been taught, "It is on earth, as it is in heaven." Do you believe heaven equates to what you are experiencing on earth right now? Take a moment, then take a look around, and whisper to your heart, welcome to heaven. Does your heart believe your whispers? Only if you believe that you reside on the planet known to man as earth. Explain to me why we are "on earth" and "in heaven." That sounds like two different experiences. To be "on" something insinuates being on top of or outside of the core of that person or place. To be "in" something insinuates an intimate relationship with the core of that person or place. It seems as if one experience is greater than the other. Now take a look around and decide if you are in an intimate relationship with life or have found yourself outside the core of your life? Are you "on earth" or "in heaven?" Or, do you simply continue to focus on hell?

In the beginning you are two separate experiences; one experience as an egg and the other experience as a sperm. You are living two individual lives through the experiences of your mother and father. Then at an appointed time, they decided to become one. In this moment of becoming one, they both contribute the knowledge of their bloodlines in its entirety. This knowledge is stored in two of the four chambers that are kept in your heart. The other two chambers of your heart consist of Gods infinite wisdom and knowledge and the very essence of you. All four of these energies combine and vibrate triggering your life to begin. This is who you are.

Getting to know you may take some time. When the outer shell cracks and I get to the core then I will discover where your allegiance lies.

Evolving 〜〜

As I venture into the genesis of the Age of
Aquarius, I prepare myself for the continuation
of this blessed life I am experiencing. Why are
so many beings focused on time? This concept
has ruined the imaginations of souls once so
great. The focus has converted to a system of
material gains. Who shall deny their wealth in a
dimension that believes as soon as you receive
it, it shall be taken away? Who has set this ideal
in motion? Who shall be brave and announce
that they are heirs to the thieves of this reality?

They have sucked the essence of your wealth and made you indebted to your own inheritance. I am the source of all. I am the way to freedom. I am the truth that shall set you free. I am the light that will guide you from the darkness. I am blessed to be chosen. I am you, the longest existing being in all creation. Let time go and you shall be free. You shall experience the eternal you for all of your being. The age has approached for your shackles to be loose, your burdens to be cast into the lake of fire, and your cares are non-existent. We have released that energy into the Pisces. It is now his cross to bear. We are electrifying, a creator within the created, an Ode to the evolved.

Acknowledgements

I first give an honor to God who is my life. In all my ways will I acknowledge Thee, as I humble myself to You. Thank you Lord for choosing me to carry forth Your will and Your love. Thank You for anointing me with the courage to share these intimate experiences and expressions that I have bared witness to, and also lived. Please accept my faith in You as a token
of appreciation for your comfort and protection during this journey.
I AM YOU.

To the reader, thank you for allowing me to share my gifts with you. I am honored that you shared your time and attention with me.   I AM YOU.

I am very gracious for the following: April Hobson, LaShanta Hampton, Peggy McClean, Sherrie Miller, Chauncey Smith and Darius Southerland for their early reviews and input for the manuscript. Your focus, and time is greatly appreciated, and our conversations were priceless. Your service will be rewarded on Earth and in Heaven, thank you. I AM YOU.

To Hommer "HomeTeam" Smith, Jr of Chicago, Illinois by way of Ita Bena, Mississippi – I sincerely thank you from the bottom of my heart for all of your contributions to the project; time, money, patience, encouragement, but most of all your love. You always found something positive to say even when I didn't want to hear it. Keep pushing me! I AM YOU.

Sherrie Miller – My Sister, you kept me focused and that is a hard task. You gave me a voice and the strength to stand up to "Corporate America." You told the TRUTH when others were afraid, and you had my back through it all. I know you have my best interest at heart, and in return for all you have poured into my life and into this book; you have my loyalty and a friend for life. Namaste, or as we say now...
I AM YOU.

LaShanta Hampton of Lewisburg, TN –
Thank you so much for being my live audience,
I read to you out loud more than I have my own
children. That's what friends do right? You
were my test market all the way across the board
– again thank you. You keep on pushing, and
keep moving forward. Your struggle will be
rewarded, believe that. Atlanta showed me that
we are more alike than I realized, we both
express our hurt through anger, but we got
through it, and smiled at the end. You had my
back when I didn't even know you – so I mean
this from deep down when I say.
I AM YOU

Brandie Lynn Bell of Tacoma, WA – I miss
you and I am so glad that God put you in my
life. You are a strong woman that has lived a
complicated life yet you always find time to see
about me. I love you more than I love myself
and I pray for you daily. You will come out of
the struggle if I have to come and snatch you out
myself. Don't ever give up on God or yourself.
God is not finished with you.
I AM YOU.

To my most valued creations, my children.
Ah'Mari, Ryann, and Genesis -
Mama loves you, though I haven't been the best
at showing it, please know that I do. Life took
me through some rough experiences but I am so
blessed to have children as resilient and loving
as you three. I thank God for your
unconditional love and patience, and trust me
when I say the best is yet to come. I promise to
do better. I'm writing these books to leave a
legacy for my family, you guys. My heart. I
AM YOU.

Finally I would like to express my love and
gratitude to my mother Peggy McClean, and my
father Robert McClean. Keep praying for me,
it's working! The last five years I have needed
you guys more than ever and you did not
disappoint. You welcomed me back home with
open arms and dealt with my anger, my
ignorance, and my bad decisions. You loved me
through it, and now I believe in love again. I
promise to represent you well, I love you both.
I AM YOU.

About The Author

TortoisWind is a freelance writer who enjoys expressing reality, actuality, philosophies, and fantasies through a creative arrangement of words.

Her childhood was split between the East Side of Tacoma, WA, and the Walking Horse Capital of the World, Shelbyville TN. Tacoma in the late 80's and most of the 90's became the stomping ground for many gangs. Many sets were represented by different cultures. Not only were the gangs represented by Blacks, Whites, Cambodians, Samoans, and Hispanics, but the entire community was diverse. Having parents that were active military and living in an area full of violence introduced TortoisWind to a protected lifestyle. She lost a few friends very young to gang violence and the problem was growing rapidly. Each summer she would visit family in Cleveland, OH and Shelbyville, TN. One summer at the age of 15 she flew into Tennessee and never returned to Tacoma. Her parents were concerned about her safety and the company she was keeping.

Shelbyville, TN - a small town about an hour south of Music City, USA (Nashville), became home for her remaining high school years. She experienced racism for the first time. She entered the school and witnessed the white kids wearing shirts with the confederate flag flying across their chest - proud. She heard a white boy yell down the hall calling a black girl a "nigger" loud and clear for everyone to hear. Teachers were present and just continued to persuade kids to get to their classrooms. The white boy was never corrected, and this moment changed her life. TortoisWind became very offended and angry. She began to question her family about what was going on in the South. This was a new experience; she was in pure cultural shock. A strong desire to "liberate" & "educate" her people came over her - she only had one plan in mind, to get out of the South. She could not understand how her people, the blacks, were okay with being so disrespected. She could not trust white people anymore.

119

It was time for a revolution.

The majority of her college years were spent at Middle Tennessee State University, where she received her degree in Business Administration with an emphasis in Marketing. In 2001, after graduation TortoisWind really began to question her position on this planet. She was working in Corporate America and hated every minute of it. The money was good, but could not ease her mind. No matter how much money she was making, it just wasn't enough. Something was missing - she wanted freedom and love.

She spent the majority of her adult years in Bluff City aka Memphis, TN. A city that seduced her the moment she arrived. Memphis was exactly what she thought she needed. It reminded her of back home in Tacoma - everyday she was surrounded by her people. She fell in and out of love, and was right back in Corporate America - now with two kids and a host of failed relationships. The violence that this city carried became disturbing.

She couldn't decipher the good from the bad -
from crooked cops to crooked pastors,
government officials going to jail, and the state
of Mississippi just two blocks up the street -
more racism. She began to notice the "good ole
boys" system in full effect at work, and now she
was convinced that she didn't like the blacks or
the whites - this was the moment she realized
she did not like herself.

After being laid off in 2009, and continuously
going through relationship struggles, she
decided to follow her passion and began to
release her pain through writing. Her connection
with the universe and the spiritual world has
influenced her first published works entitled, I
Am You.

Now her goals have evolved. It is her
personal mission to bring peace to this planet.
Peace for all people.